WARREN & Dragon

Weekend with Chewy

WARREN & Dragon

Weekend with Chewy

by Ariel Bernstein

illustrated by Mike Malbrough

VIKING

VIKING

An imprint of Penguin Random House LLC
375 Hudson Street
New York, New York 10014

First published in the United States of America by Viking,
an imprint of Penguin Random House LLC, 2018

Text copyright © 2018 by Ariel Bernstein
Illustrations copyright © 2018 by Mike Malbrough

LIBRARY OF CONGRESS CATALOGING-IN-PUBLICATION DATA IS AVAILABLE
ISBN 9780425288450

Printed in U.S.A.

1   3   5   7   9   10   8   6   4   2

✠ ✠ ✠

For Adam and Dylan. Love, Aunt Ariel

For Abe. Thanks for being a great inspiration, muse, and critic. —M.M.

✠ ✠ ✠

CONTENTS

1
Winning Chewy * 1

2
Everyone Loves Chewy * 9

3
Introductions * 15

4
Watching Chewy * 24

5
A Trillion Things to Do * 32

6
A Phone Call * 38

7
A Secret * 44

8
A Crazy Amount of Pets * 49

9
Chute of Doom * 55

10
Building the Ramp * 61

11
The Hero * 66

12
A New Secret * 72

13
Time for Chewy * 77

14
Hamster Report * 84

WARREN
& Dragon

Weekend with Chewy

1

Winning Chewy

Here I am, sitting in my second grade classroom, watching the clock move way too slowly towards two-thirty when the school bell will ring.

As I see it, I have a few options. One, I could continue to stare at the clock. But nothing is more boring than staring at a slow-moving clock. I bet even staring at a fast-moving clock would become boring after a while. Two, I could pay attention to Mrs. Tierney, my teacher. But then I would have to figure out what she's talking about. Three, I could daydream. I could become a time-traveling ninja robot sent by my dragon overlord from 15,000 years in the future to find all the marshmallows in an unsuspecting wasteland.

Four, I could ...

"Warren! Would you like to answer?" Mrs. Tierney asks. Mrs. Tierney is nice, but she's always interrupting my day by asking questions.

"Four?" I guess. I do not know what I am guessing.

"Why, yes," she says, looking surprised.

I smile back as though I am not surprised. Alison, a girl with curly red hair who sits next to me in class, is not smiling. In fact, she looks kind of angry.

"Did you totally guess that?" Alison asks.

"Yes," I say.

Alison looks madder now, even though I was just being honest.

"Congratulations, Warren," Mrs. Tierney says. "You've won the next turn to bring Chewy home for the weekend."

"Great!" I say. I do not say I have no idea who Chewy is.

"You're so lucky," Alison groans. "I still haven't had a chance to take Chewy home. He's sooo cute."

"He's not a stuffed teddy bear, is he?" I ask. Dragon, my pet dragon who is stuck at home, doesn't like stuffed teddy bears. He says they just pretend to be cute and cuddly but secretly plan to take over the world and outlaw s'mores. He gets a little crazy whenever he sees one.

Alison's eyes open wide. "He's the class pet! You know, Chewy. The hamster," she says, and points to the back of the room.

I turn around to look. How about that. There's a hamster there in a cage.

"I have to take him home for a whole weekend?" I ask.

Weekends are the best time of the week.

There's no school, no homework, and no interruptions by Mrs. Tierney. And I have this weekend all planned out. My friend Michael, who is also my next-door neighbor, said he wished we had a way to trade snacks after bedtime. Michael has great snacks like chocolate-covered bananas and jalapeño chips that would totally hit the spot right when I'm supposed to be sleeping.

I suggested building an invisible ramp between our windows. Surprisingly, we couldn't figure out a way to make a ramp invisible, so we decided to just make a regular ramp and hope people don't notice. "People" includes my parents, my sister, Ellie, Michael's two moms, his little sister, Addie, and Michael's big brother, Jayden. We're supposed to work on it this weekend, but if I have to spend the weekend taking care of Chewy, who knows if I'll have time.

"You *get* to take him home," Alison says. "Everyone's parents had to sign a form that it's okay. I wonder when it'll be my turn."

"Maybe you should study more so you can get the right answer next time," I suggest.

"But you said you guessed the answer!" Alison says.

"Yeah, but guessing is hard work," I reply.

Even Alison's curls look like they're mad at me now. I decide not to ask if she wants to come over and help me clean out Chewy's cage over the weekend.

The school bell rings, and everyone starts to pack up.

"You're going to feed him enough, right?" Alison asks. She doesn't sound mad anymore. She sounds worried.

"Of course," I say, and go to my cubby to get my jacket.

"And keep him clean and safe?" Alison adds as she follows me.

"Sure."

"And happy?"

"Why are you so worried I won't take good

care of Chewy?" I ask as I get in the line to leave.

"Because he's still in the back of the room!" Alison says.

"Oh, yeah," I say.

I walk over and lift up Chewy's cage. It's not as heavy as it looks.

MUNCH MUNCH

Chewy's eating a few food pellets in fast little bites like he's never going to get another meal.

"He's not that cute," I say.

"No one is cute when they eat," Alison replies.

I think about Dragon. He's not very cute in a cuddly way but he's still the best pet you could ever have. He knows how to joust, he plays soccer the *real* way (getting as muddy as possible without worrying about scoring goals), he likes to go camping, and he can even talk.

No one besides me ever notices Dragon talk, or walk, or do anything really, but he never seems to mind.

If Alison saw me take care of Dragon, she wouldn't be worried about Chewy. I keep Dragon very well fed. I make sure he doesn't take too many disgusting baths. And so far I've only left him behind in another time dimension once, and that was a total accident.

"Do you think Chewy can do any tricks?" I ask.

"Like what?" Alison asks.

"Roast marshmallows before gulping them down?"

"Of course he can't do that!"

"Can he build a ninja maze?"

"He's a hamster, Warren."

"Can he at least find his own way back if he gets accidentally left behind during time travel?"

Alison shakes her head.

"Then what's the point of having a hamster as a pet?" I ask.

Alison stares at me as I go to stand in line with the cage. She obviously doesn't know either.

2

Everyone Loves Chewy

My dad is waiting for me outside the school in the pick-up area. Mrs. Tierney walks over to him and motions to Chewy before giving Dad a bag of hamster food. Dad smiles like he's not sure if he's really happy. It's the same smile he gave me when I made him a necktie out of marshmallows I glued together for his birthday.

"I look forward to your report," Mrs. Tierney says to me before going back into the school. I do not say I am also looking forward to it because I don't know what report she is talking about. But now I have to write some sort of report over the weekend, too. This is just great. Maybe I can bribe Dragon with marshmallows to write one for me.

My twin sister Ellie's class lets out, and she walks over to us.

"Oh, what a cute little hamster!" Ellie squeals, and looks into the cage.

"He looks kind of ugly to me," I say.

"He's adorable," Ellie insists. "And he doesn't talk back either," she adds, looking at me.

"What's wrong with talking back?" I say. I like it when Dragon talks back to me. He says really good stuff most of the time.

"Dad, can we have a pet for real?" Ellie asks. "Not a dragon toy," she adds, shooting me a look like I was going to interrupt.

She's right, I was going to interrupt. I was going to say I don't want any new pets. Dragon is enough of a handful. Plus, he's not a toy. He's a real dragon pet, and it's not my fault no one else knows it.

"Pets are a lot of responsibility," Dad says. "You have to take care of them and feed them and make sure they don't get hurt. . . ."

"I can do all that!" Ellie pleads.

"Ellie, you hardly ever get through a whole week with the chores you already have," Dad says.

"Ellie has chores?" I ask.

"So do you!" Ellie says.

"I have chores?" I ask. "Wait, is this why I haven't gotten my allowance in forever?"

Dad looks at me and shakes his head.

Ellie glances over at me like she's thinking about something. "What if I *prove* I can be responsible?" she asks Dad.

"You can start by making your bed every morning," Dad says.

Ellie doesn't reply but walks over to me.

"Are you okay, Warren?" Ellie asks me. She

is looking at Dad as though she wants Dad to hear her.

"Yes," I say. I do not say I can't figure out why Ellie is suddenly being so nice.

"Do you need to stop and rest? Are you thirsty?" Ellie asks, and pats my head.

"No," I say, ducking her hand.

"Watch out for that puddle!" Ellie shouts, and tries to grab my arm. I move backward and start to trip before I accidentally let go of the cage.

I land hard on the ground and Chewy's cage lands on my stomach. He runs around for a moment before taking a sip of water from the attached water dispenser.

"Warren!" Dad says. "Are you okay? What happened?"

"I'm okay," I mumble while getting up.

"Are you sure, Warren?" Ellie asks. "He needs so much care and attention," she says to Dad. "Don't worry, I'll watch out for him. Just like I'd do with a real pet."

Before I can tell Ellie to stay away, Michael

walks over with one of his moms, Paula, and Addie. Michael is in first grade and I'm in second, but we still hang out at recess and after school a lot. I guess you could say he's my best human friend. Dragon is my best dragon friend, although there's not much competition.

"What's that?" Michael asks, pointing at the cage.

"A hamster," I reply.

"You get to have a dragon *and* a hamster?" Michael says in awe. Like other people, Michael isn't able to hear Dragon talk. But unlike other people, Michael still gets how awesome Dragon is.

"All I ever had was a goldfish last year," Michael adds. "He lived a good life for a couple of weeks but then I overfed him and, well, you know."

I nod in understanding. I overfeed Dragon all the time, but luckily dragons don't die because of too much food.

"We only have the hamster for the weekend," Dad quickly points out.

"Hamster boo," Addie says, and giggles as she waves to Chewy in his cage.

I do not know why everyone likes Chewy so much. All he does is run on his wheel and eat his food.

When we get to our houses, Michael tells me he's going to start thinking of ideas to build our ramp tomorrow. I say I will, too, because building a ramp to trade snacks after bedtime is way more important than taking care of a hamster or writing a report. Luckily, I have a plan.

3

Introductions

My plan is simple. All I need to do is get Dragon excited enough about Chewy so that he'll agree to watch him for me. Then I'll bribe Dragon with marshmallows so he'll write the report for me, too. And then I'll have all the time I need to plan building the ramp with Michael.

When we get inside our house, Ellie goes to the kitchen to eat a snack and Dad goes to his office room to work. He works at home as a graphic designer, and my mom works at a regular office as an engineer, but most days she gets home before bedtime. Dragon usually waits for me in my room after school, so I take the cage with Chewy in it upstairs.

As soon as I open the door I hear, "What'd you bring me?"

Dragon always expects me to bring him something on my way home from school. He says he works hard all day keeping my room safe from intruders and should be fairly compensated. Usually I forget until I see my front door and I end up grabbing a stone or leaf. But when I've remembered to look for something cool on my way home, I've found pennies and bouncing balls and even half a pack of cards once.

"I brought you this," I say, and put Chewy's cage down on the floor. "This is Chewy, the most amazing class hamster in the world." I hope I'm not overselling Chewy, but I want Dragon to think he's really special so he'll agree to watch him.

Chewy does not look up.

"Oh, I've always wanted one of those!" Dragon exclaims, and claps his claws together.

My plan is working perfectly.

Dragon hops around the cage looking at Chewy.

"Should we marinate him first in butter and cream or eat him up right now?" Dragon asks.

"What??? You can't eat him!" I shout. "I have to bring him back to school on Monday."

My plan has stopped working.

"But you said I could have him," Dragon says, looking hurt. "Plus, his name is 'Chewy.' Obviously the person who named him thinks he's supposed to be eaten."

"My teacher named him, and trust me, she doesn't want to eat him," I say, and move Chewy's cage away from Dragon and onto my desk.

Dragon hops up onto my desk chair and stares into Chewy's cage. He licks his lips, and I hear his stomach growl.

"We can't eat *any* of him?"

"No! Gross. No," I say, and shake my head.

Dragon puts two of his claws together real small. "What about just an eensy teensy little bite? With some orange-flavored glaze?"

"Not even with chocolate-flavored glaze and marshmallows melted on top," I say. "He's our guest. He'll be like a member of the family."

"I don't have a rule against eating family," Dragon says, and shrugs.

"Well, you haven't eaten any of us yet."

"That you know of," Dragon says as he raises his eyebrows.

"What's that supposed to mean?" I ask.

Dragon looks both ways like he's making sure no one is listening. "Didn't your parents ever tell you about Fluffy the cat?"

"What cat?"

"I've said too much. Besides, the only reason I didn't eat you when you came home from the hospital was because you always had drool sauce all over. I hate drool sauce."

"Oh yeah? Then why didn't you eat Ellie?" I ask.

"She was cute."

Oh, brother.

"Everyone thinks Chewy is cute, so you can't eat him either," I tell him.

"Okay, *fine*," Dragon says, and crosses his arms.

"Fine."

"I'm just, uh . . . going to the kitchen now for . . . a marshmallow," Dragon says, and starts to back out of the room. "Yeah, that's it! I'm just going to get a marshmallow."

I roll my eyes after Dragon leaves and look into Chewy's cage. He's running on his wheel like it's the most important thing in the world. He doesn't seem to have any idea he was about to be Dragon's after-school snack.

Great, now how am I supposed to get any work on the ramp done?

I see Dragon come back into the room carrying a bunch of small containers.

"What are those?" I ask, and lift them out of Dragon's grasp. "Garlic powder. Paprika. Salt and pepper?"

"The hamster is very stinky," Dragon says, and starts to turn the top of the garlic powder. "These seasonings will give him a nice aroma."

"*No, no, no!*" I shout. "Even I know these are for cooking food!"

Ellie suddenly peeks into my room. "Everything okay in here?" she asks, her eyes wide.

"Are you having fun? Do you need a rest from a long day? Do you need to eat?"

"Yes!" Dragon says. "I'm hungry, and Warren won't let me eat Chewy."

"We're fine!" I say, and push Ellie out to the hall.

"Stop being all nice!" I tell her. "It's freaking me out. Just be normal where you ignore me or get mad at me like you always do."

Ellie stomps her feet as she walks downstairs.

"Great! Be like that!" I say. Ellie turns to stick her tongue out at me. "Perfect!" I add.

I go back to my room and put the garlic powder lid back on before gathering up the spices.

"Wait. Where's the salt?" I ask Dragon.

He smiles, shrugs his shoulders, and bats his eyelashes. I pick Dragon up and see that he's been sitting on the salt container.

I take all the containers down to the kitchen and drop them into the spice rack.

"What were you doing with those?" Ellie asks

as she take out crackers from the cupboard.

"Why do you care what I'm doing all the time?" I say.

"Because I need to show Mom and Dad I can take care of you like I'd take care of a pet. Then they might get me a real pet."

"That's the dumbest idea!" I say.

"It's a brilliant idea," Ellie declares. "Do you want a cracker?" she asks as she spreads jam on some. "Pet owners need to make sure their pets are well fed."

I think about how Ellie is pretending to be a pet owner. And then I think of my own brilliant idea. "Sorry I called your idea dumb," I say.

Ellie gives me a confused look. "Why are you apologizing?" she says suspiciously.

"If you want to show Mom and Dad you can take care of a pet, why don't you just take care of Chewy this weekend?" I ask.

I can see that Ellie's thinking about it.

"I could take care of Chewy . . . but he's pretty

easy," Ellie begins. Ellie obviously doesn't have her own dragon to keep away from a hamster or she wouldn't say it was easy. "I don't want an easy pet like a hamster. I want a pet like a dog. Or a pig. I need to show Mom and Dad I can take care of something big that's smelly and eats a lot, like you. Plus, it's your responsibility to take care of Chewy this weekend. Not mine."

"I take it back," I say. "Your idea is dumb. Even if I am big and smelly—and I'm *not* smelly—I'm not a pet. Chewy is. I don't need to be fed or watched. Only real pets like Chewy need to be taken care of and . . ."

Oh no.

I am not currently watching Chewy. Dragon is currently watching Chewy. Dragon, who wants to eat Chewy.

4

Watching Chewy

I rush back upstairs.

"Are you sick?" Ellie shouts. "Should I call a doctor? Or a veterinarian?"

I ignore her and push open my door. The door to the cage is unlocked. Dragon's head is inside with his mouth open right over Chewy.

"*Stop!*" I shout.

"Oh! Hee hee . . . I was just measuring him," Dragon says innocently. "His width is one dragon mouth wide. Want me to measure his height now?"

"Step away from the hamster," I say.

Dragon squeezes his head back out of the cage.

I reach inside and carefully take Chewy out with both hands.

Chewy looks at me and blinks a few times. He doesn't look like he knows he was about to be a dragon's snack. He doesn't look like he knows much of anything.

I still don't get why anyone would want Chewy for a pet, but I am glad Dragon didn't eat him. I'm sure I'd never hear the end of it if Alison didn't get her turn to take Chewy home. I pet him on his back gently a few times and realize he's pretty soft.

"Ahem," Dragon says.

I put Chewy back in his cage and lock the door. Maybe I'll remember to pet him again later.

"So, if we can't eat him . . ." Dragon begins.

"We can't."

"Can we play hide-and-seek with him?" Dragon asks. "And, um . . . if he gets so well hidden we can't find him . . . we'll just assume he's gotten lost forever and nobody ate him," he adds very quickly.

I look at Dragon. He twiddles his claws and looks up at the ceiling, whistling.

I decide to completely give up on my plan to make Dragon hamster-sit Chewy.

Instead of spending time thinking about ideas for building the ramp, I end up watching both Dragon and Chewy carefully all afternoon and evening until nighttime. Making sure Dragon doesn't eat Chewy is a full-time job. I also don't have time for dueling practice, marshmallow experiments, or creating ninja mazes.

I don't get much sleep in either, because of all the times Dragon wakes up to sneak out of bed. Then he wakes me up and I have to put him back in. And every time Chewy hears us moving, he wakes up and starts running in his wheel.

CLICK
CLACK
CLICK
CLACK

"Listen, Dragon, you wake up one more time to eat Chewy and you're sleeping in the basement," I tell him when he wakes up for the sixth time.

"I'm not trying to eat Chewy," Dragon says as though he's offended. "I'm trying to go to the kitchen for regular food."

"I fed you all my carrots and half a pork chop from dinner," I remind him.

"You forgot to feed me dessert," he says, and pats his belly.

"I got you two cookies," I tell him.

"Yeah, but that was *before* dinner. They don't count as dessert if they're before dinner. I don't know why you brought home a second pet if you can't even take proper care of me. And how come he gets so much food?" Dragon adds, and motions to Chewy.

"It's just hamster food," I tell him. "Chewy can't eat good stuff like marshmallows and ice cream and Monster Marshmallow Madness cereal."

"Not even caramel-covered cookies with whipped cream on top?" Dragon asks.

I shake my head.

"Poor Chewy," Dragon says, looking sad. "Stuck eating hamster food in a little tiny cage. That's not a good life for a pet."

I slap my hand to my forehead.

"You know what would really hit the spot right now?" Dragon says. "Chocolate-covered bananas and jalapeño chips."

I slap my forehead again. I need to stop doing that.

"If I don't have to watch you chase Chewy around all day tomorrow I can build a ramp with Michael so we can trade for snacks like that," I say.

"Really?" Dragon asks. I'm about to reply "Really" when we both hear the bedroom door start to open.

"Everything okay in here?" Ellie whispers, shining her flashlight on me and Dragon.

"What are you doing???" I say to Ellie.

"I heard noises," Ellie replies. "Do you need more blankets?"

"No."

"Hmmm," Ellie says, as though she's thinking hard about something. "I did a bunch of research on Dad's computer on how to take care of pets. Maybe you're awake because you didn't eat enough. Or maybe you ate too much. Pets aren't allowed to have chocolate. Did you eat any chocolate?"

"Oh, dear," Dragon says. "I have been feeling light-headed recently."

Ellie doesn't wait for me to answer before she continues. "Or maybe you're awake because you need a clean living space. This room is filthy. Pets need clean living spaces. Also, they need to be groomed. Have you been groomed today? Your hair is sticking up. I don't think you've been grooming properly."

"I'm always groomed properly," Dragon says to Ellie, and dusts off his wings.

"Maybe you have to use the bathroom," Ellie suggests. "I heard pets sometimes have to use the bathroom in the middle of the night."

Dragon looks at me. "Do you have to go?"

"Leave me alone!" I yell at Ellie.

"Fine, I'll leave," Ellie grumbles. "Just tell Mom and Dad I'd know how to help a *real* pet sleep well."

I throw my pillow at the door just as Ellie's closing it.

Suddenly I hear the wheel start to turn.

"Great, now Chewy is awake again," I say.

"He probably needs a bedtime story," Dragon says. "Chewy, listen to this. Once upon a time there was a hamster that came home with a boy, and the boy's magnificent, beloved dragon. The boy could be awesome too if only he remembered to feed the dragon dessert. The hamster never got dessert because the boy was mean. The end. P.S. The dragon was always properly groomed."

Dragon yawns. "I'm exhausted now. Please be quiet so I can sleep." He curls up and soon begins snoring.

I fall back on my bed with a thud. I have no pillow. Like Chewy, I am wide awake.

Having two pets is the worst.

5

A Trillion Things to Do

The next morning, I place Chewy in his cage next to me on the floor of the kitchen while I eat breakfast. I don't like having to watch Chewy closely all the time, but I bet it's better than telling Mrs. Tierney he's gone because my dragon ate him.

I give Dragon extra helpings from my Monster Marshmallow Madness cereal in between yawning. If I can keep him well fed, then maybe he'll forget to try and eat Chewy. And then I can finally focus on building the ramp. Unless I'm forgetting something . . . but I can't remember anything else that's important.

"You okay, Warren?" my mom asks as she butters her toast.

"I didn't sleep great," I say.

"You had to go to the bathroom, didn't you?" Ellie asks. "You always have to make sure pets go to the bathroom before they sleep," she says to our dad and mom. "I know this because I'd be a super responsible and knowledgeable pet owner. Especially the owner of a pet that's big and smelly." Ellie looks at me as I pour some more cereal into my bowl. "And one that eats a lot," she adds.

My mom looks at my dad. He shrugs and takes a sip of his coffee.

"What are you up to today, Warren?" Mom asks.

"I have *so* much to do," I groan. My parents look at me with their eyebrows raised. "I have to watch Chewy all the time to make sure he's okay *and* I have about a hundred things to do."

"It's more like a billion," Dragon interrupts.

"A billion things to do . . ." I begin.

"No, more like a trillion," Dragon says.

"A trillion things . . ."

"At least ten things to do."

"I have a *lot* to get done," I say, and toss Dragon some more cereal so he'll eat instead of interrupting me.

"Do you need any supervision, Warren?" Ellie asks innocently. "I can take you places, like on a walk. A walk is always good exercise for a pet," she tells our parents.

"I do not need to take a walk," I say. "You, however, can take a hike. . . ."

"Hiking is a great idea!" Ellie exclaims. "Pets love hiking with their owners." Again, Ellie keeps glancing at Mom and Dad when she's talking. "You just need to bring water, and a pooper scooper, and maybe a couple of pet snacks."

"Like chocolate-covered bananas?" Dragon asks hopefully.

"I'm not going anywhere with you," I say to Ellie. "I'm also not going anywhere with a pooper scooper. And I'm definitely not going anywhere with you *and* a pooper scooper."

"Fine, but you'll miss out on some great exercise, which all pets need," Ellie says, like she's an expert or something.

"Fine by me," I say. "Like I said, I already have a ton of stuff to get done today."

"Sounds like a busy day," Mom says. "Wait, what *exactly* are you planning to do today?"

She looks worried. Maybe it's because of all the other weekends where my and Dragon's plans ended up with walls needing new paint.

"Uh, take care of Chewy?" I say innocently.

"That won't involve any food on the walls, right?" Mom asks.

"Of course not," I say. "A ramp isn't a wall."

"Good," Mom says. "Wait, what ramp?"

"Can't talk, Mom. Too many things to do!" I say as I lift up Chewy's cage and begin to leave the kitchen with Dragon.

"Including that report," my dad says right before we make it out the door.

Argh. The report! I completely forgot about it.

"I still have to write that stupid report," I tell Dragon when we get out of the kitchen. "I don't even know what it's supposed to be about."

"You have to write a report the same weekend you bring Chewy home, huh?" Dragon says and taps his belly thoughtfully. "Maybe the report is supposed to be *about* Chewy?"

"That kinda makes sense," I say.

"Or maybe the report is supposed to be about pets you already have and how they're so much better than a hamster."

"I don't think so."

"Or *maybe* the report is supposed to be about why dragons make better pets than any other pet in the world. There are limitless examples you could cite in your report. For example, we're the most friendly, the most humble, the most helpful . . ."

"I definitely don't think so."

"Or *maybe* . . ."

"Look, I don't know for sure what the report is supposed to be about," I say. "But I do know someone who would know."

6

A Phone Call

Dragon follows me into Dad's office room. I put Chewy's cage down on the floor.

"Who are you calling?" Dragon asks as I pick up the phone. He's climbed up to the edge of the office desk to stand near the phone.

"Alison," I reply. "I just have to find her number in the school directory book."

"Oooh, a phone call!" Dragon says, and smiles a really big, swoony smile. "Girls love it when you call them. It's so old-fashioned."

"Wait, she's not gonna think I'm calling because I want to, is she?" I ask. I start to feel worried. "I'm only calling because I have to."

"I don't know," Dragon says. "I heard of a boy who called a girl once, and the next thing you know they were married and opened a marshmallow bakery together."

"Just because of a phone call?" I ask.

"Yep."

I shudder.

I find Alison's number and punch in the numbers.

"Hello?" A woman answers. I'm guessing it's Alison's mom.

"This is Warren Nesbitt. Can I speak to Alison?" I say.

"You forgot to say 'please,'" Dragon says.

"Can I please speak to Alison?" I say.

"You forgot to say 'May I,'" Dragon says.

I put my hand over Dragon's mouth. He gives it a nip and I take my hand away.

"Sure. Hold on one moment," Alison's mom says.

"Hello?" I hear Alison say.

"Hi, Alison. This is Warren. First of all, you need to know that I didn't want to call you but I have to even though I'd rather drink a smoothie made of anchovies and olives. No, wait. I'd rather stand outside and get soaked in rain and then get struck by lightning. No, wait. I'd rather get eaten by a six-eyed ginormous wasp. No, wait—"

I look at the phone.

"What happened?" Dragon asks.

"She hung up on me."

"You should have stopped after the smoothie

made of anchovies and olives," Dragon says.

He's probably right.

"You know, opening a marshmallow bakery doesn't sound so bad," Dragon says thoughtfully. "You could have marshmallow pie, marshmallow doughnuts, marshmallow pudding . . ."

I press the numbers into the phone again.

"*What?!?*" Alison says as soon as she answers.

"I'm sorry, okay? I'm just calling to ask about the report I have to write this weekend."

"You mean the report about Chewy?"

"So the report *is* supposed to be about Chewy," I say.

Dragon does a little jig as he points to himself

and says, "I was right. Genius here. Always listen to me. I know everything. I know—" Dragon loses his balance and tips over the side of the desk.

"What was that noise?" Alison asks after Dragon crashes onto the floor.

I reach out with my free hand and help Dragon up. He's a little woozy.

"Something fell, but it'll be okay. I really have to write a report about Chewy?"

"*Of course* the report is about Chewy," Alison says. "You have to write about how much he eats, how long he sleeps, if you like having him as a pet . . . all that stuff."

I write down what's she's saying on a notepad. "Okay, eating, sleeping . . . nothing about anyone trying to eat him. . . ."

"*What?!?*" Alison shrieks.

I look at the phone.

"What happened?" Dragon asks as he massages his head. "Why is she yelling? Did an invisible ninja come out of nowhere and push her onto the floor, too?"

"She hung up on me again," I say.

Dragon gives a sad pout. "Does this mean you're not gonna open a marshmallow bakery?"

7

A Secret

A couple of minutes later the doorbell rings. I hear my mom greeting Michael at the door.

I turn to Dragon. "Listen," I say quickly, "if you write that report for me, I'll give you all the marshmallows I can find. Plus, I'll ask Michael for chocolate-covered bananas that you can have. If Michael and I get the ramp built in time, you can even get the bananas after bedtime tonight when we're supposed to be sleeping."

Dragon licks his lips. "How about marshmallows, chocolate-covered bananas, *and* jalapeño chips?" he asks.

I roll my eyes. "Fine, sure. I'll get you all those snacks. So will you write the report while Michael and I build the ramp?"

"The report has to be about Chewy?"

"Yes. You just have to write about him eating and sleeping and stuff."

"Why can't you just write the report on Sunday?" he asks.

"Because, if we're building the ramp today, then tomorrow..."

"You'll need a full day to add improvements like a water tower?" Dragon asks. "Turn it into an amusement park ride?"

"No," I reply. "If Michael and I build it today, then tomorrow we'll have to spend the day figuring out how to hide it from people. Especially parent- and sibling-type people."

"Oh, right," Dragon says. "That will take all day."

"So, do we have a deal?" I ask.

"Deal," he says, and extends a claw. We shake

on it. My plan is back on. "I'll write you the best hamster report ever written," Dragon adds.

I hand Dragon a small pad of paper from the desk and a pen.

"Warren," I hear my mom call. "Michael's here." I walk over to the front door.

"Hi, Michael," I say.

"Hi!" Michael says excitedly. He's carrying a notepad, a pen, measuring tape, duct tape, and a jump rope.

"What are you two up to today?" Mom asks, eyeing Michael's assortment of things.

"Something really cool!" Michael says. "But I can't tell you what it is, because it's a secret."

"You can't even give me a little hint?" Mom asks Michael in her super-nice voice. I know that voice. She uses it when she's pretending she doesn't care what your answer is, but she really does. Because if you give her the wrong answer, then her voice becomes not so nice. But Michael doesn't know that, so I interrupt.

"Mom, does it matter what we're doing as long as we're not sitting inside playing on your iPad all day?" I say.

I can see my that my mom is thinking about what I said. "I guess it's good you'll be playing outside . . ." she begins.

"Don't worry, Mom," Ellie says. I turn to see

her standing behind me. "I'll watch over the pets' playdate. I mean, the boys' playdate."

"That's, uh, nice of you, Ellie?" Mom says, confused.

"You can't watch us," I say.

"Why not?" Ellie asks.

"Because I already have to watch Chewy and that actually takes time. And you're going to slow us down even more by pretending we're pets and telling us what to do. We'll never finish our super-secret project with all these distractions."

Dragon pulls at my shirt to get my attention. "I can't work on the report with too many distractions," he says.

"We have very important things to get done," I declare, and fold my arms. "No more distractions."

The doorbell rings.

8

A Crazy Amount of Pets

Since Michael is closest, he opens the door. It's Alison, and she's huffing and puffing. Her face is almost as red as her hair. She looks like she ran over to my house.

"Hi, Alison," Mom says, sounding confused again. "Do you and Ellie have a playdate today?"

"Mom, I wouldn't schedule a playdate while I'm watching pets," Ellie says. "I mean, the boys. I'm not irresponsible like that."

"Is he okay?" Alison asks, looking down at Chewy.

"I'm a little parched since Warren didn't give me any orange juice at breakfast, but otherwise doing okay," Dragon says, and flexes his dragon muscles. "See, I'm in tip-top shape."

I don't tell Dragon that I don't think Alison is talking about him.

"Chewy's fine," I tell her.

"I told my parents it was a pet emergency," Alison says as she steps inside the house. "They understand because we have a lot of pets and there are always lots of animal emergencies."

"How many pets do you have?" I ask.

"Any dragons?" Dragon adds.

Alison holds up her hands to check off her fingers. "Let's see, we have two dogs, Ralph and Lenny. Four cats. Really three cats and one kitten. Mittens, Guppy, Lexie, and Captain Blotch. Captain Blotch is the kitten. One gerbil named Joe. Three fish, Riley, Smiley, and Kylie. There were four but you know how it is with fish."

Dragon nods his head in understanding. "That's why you have to get dragons. We live a really long time. I'm a hundred and twenty-two and I don't look a day over thirty-five."

"There's also a deer that always comes into our backyard," Alison continues. "My parents say I can't keep him as a pet but I named him Bobby anyway."

"That's a crazy amount of pets," I say. I do not say I feel kind of silly for complaining about having two pets for just one weekend.

Alison crouches down to look at Chewy in his cage. He's running around in his wheel. Dragon stands by Alison and begins telling her about all the benefits of having a dragon as a pet. "We never get fleas, we can toast all your marshmallows to a perfect crisp, we sleep through the night as long as you feed us dessert...."

I crouch down next to Alison and look at Chewy, too.

"You've got to be easier than having two dogs and four cats," I tell Chewy. He doesn't say anything. I take it that he agrees with me.

"Are you okay?" Alison whispers to Chewy. "I'm here to help you."

"Jeez, I only tried to eat him once or maybe ten times," Dragon huffs. "And I'm not even trying to eat him anymore!" Dragon makes notes on the pad. "The handsome dragon has decided to stop trying to eat Chewy. Chewy is both relieved and grateful."

"Warren, maybe we should start working on our . . . uh . . . secret thing," Michael says, and smiles nervously at my mom.

"Whatever it is, make sure you don't make a mess," Mom says. "Alison, I'm going to call your parents to see how long they want you to stay."

Mom leaves and Alison stands up. "What secret thing?" Alison asks.

"Doesn't anybody know what *secret* means?" I say.

"I bet it means something that you and Michael are going to do that's going to make a big mess," Ellie declares. "But I'll be watching you both."

"No, you won't," I say.

"Yes, I will. And you can't stop me. I'm going to prove I'd make a responsible pet owner whether you act like a good pet or a bad one."

Alison looks at me. "Is everyone in your family this . . . uh . . . interesting?"

I think about it for a moment.

"Yes," I say.

Alison leans back down and looks into Chewy's cage. "It's a good things I'm here," she tells him.

9

Chute of Doom

I decide to ignore Ellie. "Come on," I say to Michael. "Let's get started."

"Can I come?" Alison asks. "I've never seen anything secret being made before."

I raise my eyebrows at her. Alison tagging along in addition to Ellie is the worst idea.

"I can help watch Chewy," Alison says, and lifts up his cage. "As long as Chewy's cage is on a flat surface in the shade, he'll be okay."

I change my mind. Alison tagging along is the best idea. With Alison watching Chewy, and Dragon writing my report, Michael and I might actually build the ramp today.

"Just don't slow us down," I tell Alison.

She nods and follows me and Michael. We walk over to the side of Michael's house where his bedroom window faces mine from the second floor. Ellie follows us, too, but stands a little behind.

Dragon talks aloud as he writes notes on his pad. "While unaccustomed to traveling to the great outdoors, Chewy craves adventure. Still trapped inside his tiny cage, Chewy looks around for objects that will help him with his daring escape. The tall, red curly-haired lass is standing guard. He will have to use all his abilities to get past her watchful gaze."

"Do you have any supplies?" Michael asks as he places the notepad, pen, measuring tape, duct tape, and jump rope on the ground.

"Um . . . not really," I admit sheepishly. "I meant to start planning yesterday, but things got a little crazy." I give Dragon a look but he's not paying attention.

Dragon's writing more on the notepad.

"Chewy's reasons for escape are numerous. One, he longs to be as free as a dragon. Two, he desires to eat more than boring hamster food. Like marshmallows, and chocolate-covered bananas. Maybe both at the same time. Three, he lives in a tiny hamster cage. Who wants to live in a tiny hamster cage? Nobody, that's who. Not even a tiny hamster like Chewy."

"That's okay," Michael says, and points to some boxes stacked near the end of his driveway. "We should figure out what kind of ramp we want to build."

"Right," I say. I do not say I did not think there was more than one kind of ramp.

"What's the ramp for?" Alison asks.

"To trade snacks at night when we're supposed to be sleeping," Michael replies, then immediately covers his mouth. "But that's a secret!" He adds, "So . . . don't tell anyone, okay?"

"You're going to build a ramp between your houses?" Alison asks.

"Yeah," I say.

"And it's going to be a secret?"

"Yeah," Michael says.

"This should be interesting," Alison says, and sits on the ground next to Chewy's cage.

"So, what kind of ramp are we gonna build?" Michael asks me.

"A good one?" I answer.

"I watched a lot of house-improvement shows on TV yesterday after school so I've got some great ideas!" Michael says. "First, there's the basic, lightweight ramp that'll only be used for exchanging snacks. Or we could do a bigger, kid-size ramp. We can use that one to slide over into each other's rooms. That'll be super useful for whenever we get grounded."

"You're gonna get grounded for building a ramp," Ellie interrupts, and shakes her head. "Some pets are really crazy. . . ."

"We're not pets!" I shout at her before turning back to Michael. "What other ramp options are there?"

"There's the environmentally friendly ramp

that uses solar panels. But I don't know where to get a solar panel or how they work. I'm not even really sure what a solar panel is," Michael admits. "So maybe that's not an option. Finally, and I saved the best for last, there's the chute-of-doom ramp."

"That one!" Dragon cries out. "Make the chute-of-doom ramp!" He returns to scribbling on the notepad. "Chewy vastly prefers the chute-of-doom ramp."

"Maybe we can grease it with butter so everything slides on it super fast," Michael says excitedly. "Also, we can make the ramp all rickety like it might fall at any moment."

"That's a terrible idea," Alison says. "Why would you want to make a ramp that looks like it could fall at any moment?"

"For fun!" Michael and I say at the same time. We look at each other.

"Chute-of-doom ramp?" Michael says with a smile.

"Chute-of-doom ramp," I agree.

10

Building the Ramp

Michael and I start collecting anything we can find in our backyards that could help us make the ramp. I bring over a couple of deck chairs to stand on so we can reach our windows. Michael brings over some empty cardboard boxes from the recycling pile. We also gather a ton of sticks, leaves, and pebbles.

We work all morning on the ramp. Ellie reminds us a couple of times to take bathroom and snack breaks. I don't like it when she tells us to do stuff, although the snack breaks are always a good idea.

Dragon spends his time writing more on the notepad, but I don't see what he's writing. I'm too busy taping the pieces of cardboard together and applying sticks, pebbles, and leaves all over. Chewy seems to be okay with Alison, so I don't check on him much.

It's finally time to connect the ramp to both of our window ledges. I stand on one chair near my house while Michael props up one end of the ramp. He's having trouble lifting it up to me.

"A little higher over there," Alison says.

"No, over there," Ellie says.

"Where?" Michael asks. One edge of the cardboard is covering his vision and he can't see anything.

"A little help?" I call out to Alison and Ellie.

"I'm not helping you get into trouble," Ellie says, and crosses her arms.

"This is too sad to watch," Alison declares, and stands up. "I'll help you."

Alison takes an end of the ramp and lifts it up with Michael. I secure the end to the ledge with duct tape. We try to repeat the process at the other end near Michael's window ledge. The ramp is almost long enough, but not quite.

"Oh no," Michael says. "We didn't measure right. We have to start from the beginning. I don't think we have enough cardboard boxes to make another ramp right now."

"You don't have to completely rebuild it," Alison says. "Just measure the length you're missing and add on more cardboard to the end."

"Good idea!" Michael says.

"Yeah, thanks," I add. Alison smiles.

With Alison's help, we measure the remaining length needed, cut out the right amount of cardboard, and add it to the ramp.

Alison and Michael lift the updated ramp to me while I'm standing on the chair. I'm able to attach it to the ledge in front of Michael's window.

"Yes!" Michael exclaims.

"It worked!" I say. "Let's test it out. What snack should we try out first?"

"Marshmallows," Dragon says.

"Bubble gum," Michael says.

"Banana bread," Alison says.

"What kind of food does a pet need after bedtime?" Ellie says. "What kind of pet food does Chewy . . . Um . . . Warren?"

"Yeah?" I say.

"Where's Chewy?"

We all look down at Chewy's cage. The door is open and Chewy is nowhere to be seen.

11

The Hero

"Where'd he go?" I cry out, looking around frantically. "I don't see Chewy anywhere."

"Poor Chewy!" Alison says. "He's probably hungry and scared. We have to find him!"

"I can't believe you lost Chewy," Ellie says, and shakes her head. "You'd better find him or you're gonna get in trouble."

"Oh yeah," I say, walking up to Ellie in a huff. "Well, you're supposed to be watching *me*. And you didn't make sure I was watching Chewy. So this is all your fault."

"It's not all my fault!" Ellie argues.

"It's a little bit your fault," I say.

Ellie frowns as she looks around the side of the house. "I guess I didn't do a great job watching you," she says. "Poor Chewy. I'll check the patio."

"I'll check our backyards," Michael says.

"I'll help Michael," Alison declares, and follows him.

"Here, Chewy," Ellie calls out as she begins walking around our house. "Here, Chewy."

I am looking under the chair I was standing on when I see Dragon writing on the notepad.

"What are you doing?" I ask.

"This report has suddenly become an epic tale of adventure, daring, escape, action!" Dragon says, and scribbles with a flourish.

I take the notepad and pen out of Dragon's claws and put them behind my back. He looks at me in suprise.

"Did you open Chewy's cage?" I ask.

"That depends," Dragon replies. "Do you mean 'open' as in, did I open the cage door and set Chewy free?"

I raise my eyebrow.

"Then yes, I opened the cage."

"You're crazy!" I exclaim.

Dragon looks to either side of him before looking back at me. "You're just realizing this?"

"Listen," I say, and poke Dragon on his snout. "If we don't find Chewy, I'm going to get in a lot of trouble. With my parents and my teacher and probably the whole class. So we need to find Chewy or no more marshmallows."

Dragon gasps. "Ever?" he says.

"Ever," I reply.

"This report has gotten very dark," Dragon says. "Luckily, every report needs a hero!" Before I can react, Dragon reaches behind me and grabs the notepad and pen. He runs off and I quickly follow.

Dragon runs up trees and under bushes. No sign of Chewy. He crawls through the gutter and comes out with leaves all over. I help Dragon as

he shakes them off. Still no sign of Chewy.

Dragon takes the notepad and writes a few lines. "The hero's quest is thus far thwarted. Maybe if he had some marshmallows to renew his energy, he'd be successful." Dragon looks up at me and blinks his eyes a few times.

"No marshmallows until we find Chewy," I say. Dragon huffs.

Michael, Alison, and Ellie come running to meet us in the front yard.

"We checked the swing set, my tree house, the recycling bins, everywhere," Michael says, and throws his hands up in the air.

"I checked all over the patio and in the flower patch," Ellie says. "He wasn't there. Having a pet who has a pet is so hard."

"I don't know where Chewy could be," Alison says, her eyes becoming teary. "He's not outside anywhere."

"Uh, guys? Maybe he's not outside," Michael says, and points to the front door. It's open.

"Who left the front door open after the last snack break?" Ellie demands.

"It doesn't matter," I say. I do not say it might have been me who forgot to close the door after the last snack break. "Let's go find Chewy!"

12

A New Secret

We all rush into the house together and run straight into my dad.

"What's going on, guys?" he asks as he puts his hands in front of him to slow us down.

"It's a secret," Michael says.

"Is this a new secret or the one from this morning?" my dad muses.

"Um, a new one," Michael says. "But it's definitely not a really bad secret that would get us all in a lot of trouble."

"And it's not a secret that would prove I can't be a responsible pet owner," Ellie says.

My dad raises his eyebrows. "So what kind of secret is it?"

"An educational one," Alison replies.

We all look at her in surprise.

"Well, it's kind of true," she says, and shrugs. "Everything can be educational if you think about it."

"Do you need any help with your educational secret?" my dad asks.

"No," we all reply in unison.

"Carry on then," he says, and steps aside.

Michael and Alison sprint toward the kitchen. Ellie opens the door to the basement and heads downstairs. Dragon and I rush up the stairs.

Chewy isn't in the hall bathroom, my parents' bedroom, or Ellie's room.

"We only have one more room to check," I say with a sigh.

"You're really worried about getting in trouble, huh?" Dragon asks.

I think about Chewy and where he could be.

He won't have any food or water, or his little wheel. I wonder if he's scared.

"I always get in trouble," I say. "I'm more worried about Chewy. I thought we'd find him by now. It'll be all my fault if he's not okay."

"I thought it was my fault," Dragon says.

I look at the floor and shake my head. "No, it's my fault. I'm the one who was responsible for Chewy. Not you. Not Ellie. Just me."

Dragon's stomach growls. "Does that mean I can have a marshmallow?"

"That means we still have to find Chewy first."

As we head to my room, Ellie, Alison, and Michael come up the stairs empty-handed.

"Alison thought Chewy might return to someplace he's familiar with," Ellie tells us. "I told her Chewy was in your room all last night and yesterday after school."

We all go in my room and start to search. It's a little embarrassing to see Alison stumble across my goo collection, especially because some of it's pretty old. But mostly I'm glad I'm not looking for Chewy on my own.

"Hey," I say. Everyone stops where they're searching to look at me. "Thanks for helping me look for Chewy. I don't know if we're going to find him . . ."

"Warren," Alison says, pointing at me.

"I'll have to tell my parents now," I say.

"No, Warren!" Alison says, now jabbing her finger toward me.

"I know, it's my fault!" I say. "It's all my fault. Okay?"

"Uh, Warren?" Ellie says, standing by Alison. "She's pointing behind you."

I turn around and see that behind me is my window. The window is open. And beyond the window is the chute-of-doom ramp. And on the chute-of-doom ramp is Chewy, looking like he's about to fall off of it.

13

Time for Chewy

Lots of things happen at once. Alison covers her mouth, then her eyes, and then tries to cover her whole face.

Ellie says, "There's nothing about this in the pet owner manuals."

Michael runs out of the room, shouting, "I gotta catch him when he falls!"

I reach my hands out of the window as far as they'll go over the ramp.

"Come here, Chewy," I say, but he's too far away to grab. "Come here, and you can have as many food pellets as you want." Chewy moves a little forward, but the chute wobbles from side to side.

"Wait!" I say. "Stay there, Chewy. Don't move!"

Michael is now underneath the chute with his hands up. Alison comes rushing around the side of the house and I see she's brought my bed pillow, which she lays on the ground.

"In case we don't catch him," she tells Michael. Michael grimaces. "I can't even see where Chewy is up there. Oh, there he is!" Alison exclaims. "Wait, that's not Chewy. That's the dragon doll. What's that doing up there?"

I look over and see that Dragon is now on the chute in front of Chewy.

"I can't believe she still calls me a doll," Dragon bristles. He then turns his attention to Chewy. "Look, Chewy, I hope this has all been fun for you. Your life was super boring and now it's super interesting. We got some great material for Warren's report," Dragon adds, and pats the notepad. "But I need marshmallows, Chewy, which means you have to return to your normal, safe little life in a cage. Maybe you can visit every once in a while and we'll play ninja warriors. I won't even try to eat you when you visit."

Chewy just looks at Dragon.

"This way, Chewy," Dragon says, and extends a claw. Chewy moves toward Dragon. I can't believe it. Dragon's actually getting Chewy to follow him.

"Come on, little fella," Dragon says as he slowly leads Chewy toward my window. They're

inching closer, closer, and then ... the chute begins to swing side to side. Dragon clutches onto the chute with his leg claws, but Chewy doesn't know to hang on anywhere.

"Be careful, Chewy!" Alison screams. Michael runs around underneath, trying to find where Chewy is in case he falls.

"Please don't fall!" Ellie yells to Chewy. "I don't know what to do if a pet falls!"

Chewy is about to topple over the side when Dragon drops the notepad and reaches for Chewy with

Toss

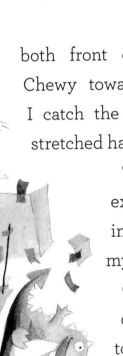

both front claws. Dragon swings Chewy toward the window where I catch the hamster with my out-stretched hands.

"Oh my goodness!" Ellie exclaims as I take Chewy inside and put him on my bed. "I can't believe Chewy pushed off the dragon so he could jump to you! That was the scar-iest thing ever."

I hear a loud thud, and Dragon scampers through the window soon after.

"Don't worry, I'm okay," he says in between deep breaths. "But the notepad didn't make it.

And the chute definitely didn't make it."

"All that matters is that Chewy's okay," I say, and gently pat Chewy on the back.

"What is going on here?" I hear my mom say. She's standing at my bedroom door with my dad, Alison, and Michael right behind her.

My dad brushes past everyone to look out the window.

"What is that . . . thing hanging down from your window ledge?" he says. "Is that card-board?"

"It's a secret," Michael says.

"It's an educational experiment," Alison says.

"It's the reason why I never, ever want a pet," Ellie says emphatically. "Pets are way too much work. Plus, how am I supposed to know what to do if a pet goes on a chute-of-doom ramp?"

"Chute-of-doom ramp?" my mom asks.

"It's kind of a funny story," I say.

"Good. You can tell us after you clean up whatever's on the side of our house," my dad says.

"That's another thing," Ellie says. "Pets make big messes."

"All pets *always* make messes," Alison says. "It's no biggie. You just have to clean up."

"Alison's right. We'll clean it all up," I say.

My parents look at me, surprised.

"We'll clean up?" Dragon says, also surprised. I guess it's because it's the first time I've said I'll clean up without being asked ten times by my parents first.

"If we clean up, we still have the rest of today and tomorrow for fun stuff."

"And time to take care of Chewy," Alison adds.

"I will definitely make time for Chewy," I say, and hold him tightly in my hands.

How about that. Sometimes there's time for everything.

"And time to write that report," my mom adds.

Blergh!

14

Hamster Report

Against my will, I have returned to the waste-land. This time I bring along my tiny ninja side-kick, Chewy the fearless warrior hamster robot. I send Chewy off to forage for marshmallows in the barren lands, but he is quickly trapped in a cage.

I try my best but I cannot save him. The locals, especially the big one who is obviously their leader, insist on keeping Chewy trapped there forever. I tell Chewy I will bring him food pellets and begin to retreat, but their leader captures me as well.

"Warren?" Mrs. Tierney asks. "Are you ready to give your report?"

"Report?"

"Your report on taking care of Chewy over the weekend," Mrs. Tierney says, looking concerned. "You did write one, didn't you?"

"Oh, yeah," I say, and shuffle through my backpack. I pull out the report, stand up, and walk to the front of the classroom.

I look around at the class and clear my throat. "Chewy liked to eat hamster food and apples and even some lettuce. He drank lots of water. Chewy slept a lot in the day and played a lot at night." I see Mrs. Tierney nod her head. My report is going great. "He did not fall asleep to bedtime stories, even really good ones."

"You read him bedtime stories?" Nicky says, and snorts. Some other kids giggle.

"For your information, they were the best bedtime stories ever told," I say. "But you'll never hear them, because you are not a hamster."

Nicky looks confused. I continue. "Chewy is one dragon mouth–width wide and half a dragon tail long."

"What?" Anika says. "Why's that in your report? How do you even measure a hamster with a dragon?"

"I don't have room in my report to explain every little thing," I tell Anika. "Maybe if you spent less time paying attention in school, and more time daydreaming, you'd learn important stuff, too."

Mrs. Tierney looks like she wants to say something, but she just opens her mouth and then closes it again.

"Anyway," I say loudly. "When Chewy was awake, he was very brave. He was good at not getting eaten, which was good. Best of all, Chewy was great at escaping the chute-of-doom ramp."

Now a whole bunch of kids are raising their hands, wanting to ask me stuff. I look at Mrs. Tierney triumphantly. Most of these reports are so boring that I imagine being a time-traveling ninja robot as soon as the kid starts talking. But my report is obviously super interesting, because I have everyone's attention.

"We'll save questions for after the report," I say, and hold up a hand. "My sister, Ellie, does not want to keep Chewy as a pet because now she doesn't want to have any pets, especially people pets. But others in my house would like to keep Chewy as a pet. I am one of those people." I look around the room again. "Okay, that's the end."

Everyone is waving their hands and shouting out questions, but Mrs. Tierney shushes the room as she walks up to the front. "Uh, thank you, Warren," she says, "for that very interesting and rather informative report. Maybe too informative."

"You're welcome," I say, and go back to my desk where I sit next to Alison.

"That was surprisingly not terrible," Alison says.

"Thanks!" I say.

"We'll have another contest this Friday to see who gets to bring Chewy home next," Mrs. Tierney tells the class.

"Oh, I hope I win!" Alison says. "I can't wait to introduce Chewy to all my animals."

"They won't try to eat him, will they?" I ask.

"Of course not," Alison says.

"When it's your turn to take Chewy, you'll feed him enough?"

"Warren, you know I will."

"And you'll make sure he has fun?"

"Yes."

"And you'll make sure he doesn't get lost again?"

Alison looks at me and shakes her head, but she's still smiling.

"Warren, when it's my turn to take Chewy, do

you want to come over and help me take care of him?"

I smile.

I make a deal with a redheaded local to visit Chewy at her home base at an unspecified date. When it's time, I will bring along marshmallows and a dragon.

Turn the page to
read a chapter of

WARREN
& Dragon
100 Friends

WARREN & Dragon

100 Friends

by Ariel
Bernstein

Illustrated by Mike Malbrough

How to Make Friends

"Ugh. How am I going to pack all this in one week?" I say, looking at my room.

"Don't pack everything," Dragon says. "Just the good stuff. Like me."

I lift up a plastic green tarantula and a blob of gooey fake ghost slime and toss them into a box.

"Everything I have is good."

"What about this?" Dragon asks, holding up the broken half of a blue crayon.

"I might need half of a blue crayon one day." I throw the crayon in the box and it splits into two more halves.

"Dragon, I need to make more friends than Ellie when we move."

"Why do you want to make more friends? You have me," Dragon says.

"Ellie's always right about everything," I say, and Dragon nods his head because he knows what I'm talking about. Ellie was right when she said the tub would flood if I put too many ninja toys near the drain, even though they really needed water training. She was right when she said my stomach would hurt from eating so many marshmallows at once, even though it was Dragon's idea to challenge me and he won anyway. And Ellie was right when she said if I didn't put on enough sunblock I'd get red, even though it was more important to help Dragon prepare for his annual fire-breathing exam that day. Dragon and I both ended up getting burned.

"I want to be right just one time," I say. "So how do I make friends?"

"That's easy," Dragon says. "When I want to make a new friend, I tell them they can either be my friend or I'll burn down their village."

"Dad says we're moving to a new town, not a village."

"Oh, that's a shame."

I find a smushed chocolate chip cookie under a pile of books. I break it in two and give half to Dragon.

"Still fresh," he says.

"I think it's only from a couple of months ago," I say.

"You know, people like compliments," Dragon says after licking the melted chocolate off his claws. "You can make friends fast by giving out compliments. Try it on me."

"Okay. You're very . . . dragon-y."

"That's not a compliment."

"You're slimy?"

"Also not a compliment. Compliments are supposed to make a friend feel good."

"Um . . . you smell especially smoky today."

"A little better. And?"

"Your tail is super spiky and a nice shade of green."

"It's not *just* green. It's emerald green!"

"Oh. Really?"

"Hmm ... forget the compliments. Let's think of something else."

I pick up three monsters glued together. "I don't play with these anymore."

"They're my bodyguards," Dragon says.

"What do you need bodyguards for?"

"I'm very desirable."

"Okay," I say, and put the monsters into the box. "Hey! How did *we* become such good friends?"

"We have lots in common," Dragon says. "We both love marshmallows. We enjoy seeing how fast things can go down staircases. We like training worms to be ninja warriors. We're really good at getting out of bath time. And we both love marshmallows."

"So all I need is to find a hundred kids who love all the same stuff as me."

"Yes."

"I'm never going to make any friends," I say.

❉ ❉ ❉

That night I dream about living in the new town. I show all the kids at school a magic show where I stuff my books into my backpack and then pull out a flying robot rabbit. Everybody wants to be my friend, but I only agree to be friends with the first hundred of them. Ellie sulks because no one wants to be her friend.

All of my friends want to sit next to me in class. At lunch my friends give me marshmallows so I'll eat next to them. At recess my friends play whatever I want. When I come home I hang out with Dragon, but Mom calls me to the front door. My one hundred friends are waiting to play with me.

"Leave me alone! I need a break!" I yell. All one hundred friends run away.

"I told you you'd never be able to make friends," Ellie says with a smirk.

I wake up next to a snoring Dragon.

"I'll show her," I say out loud. "I will make friends this time."

Coming soon!

WARREN & Dragon
Volcano Deluxe